GOLDILOCKS AND THE THREE BEARS

&

Illustrated by
Ben Mahan

Troll Associates

Library of Congress Cataloging in Publication Data
Main entry under title:

Goldilocks and the three bears.

   SUMMARY: Lost in the woods, a tired and hungry little
girl finds the home of the three bears where she helps
herself to food and goes to sleep.
   [1. Folklore.   2. Bears—Fiction]   I. Mahan, Benton.
II. Three bears.
PZ8.1.G623   398.2'1   80-27631
ISBN 0-89375-470-6
ISBN 0-89375-471-4 (pbk.)

GOLDILOCKS AND THE THREE BEARS

Once upon a time, there were three bears—Papa Bear, Mama Bear, and Baby Bear. They all lived together in their own little house in the woods.

Every morning, they each had a bowl of porridge. Papa Bear had a great big bowl, because he was the biggest. Mama Bear had a middle-sized bowl, because she was middle-sized. And Baby Bear had a wee little bowl, because he was smallest.

They each had a chair to sit in. Papa Bear had a great big chair. Mama Bear had a middle-sized chair. And Baby Bear had a wee little chair.

And they each had a bed to sleep in. Papa Bear had a
great big bed. Mama Bear had a middle-sized bed. And
Baby Bear had a wee little bed.

One morning, the three bears poured their porridge
into their bowls, but it was too hot to eat. So while the
porridge was cooling, the three bears went outside for a
walk.

It happened that a little girl had lost her way in the woods. She was called Goldilocks, because her hair was the color of gold. Now when she saw the bears' house, she walked right up to it and looked in the window.

Then she peeked through the keyhole. Finally, seeing that no one was home, she lifted the latch and went inside.

There on the table were the three bowls of porridge. Goldilocks tasted the porridge in Papa Bear's great big bowl. It was too hot for her. Next, she tasted the porridge in Mama Bear's middle-sized bowl. It was too cold for her. Then she tasted the porridge in Baby Bear's wee little bowl. It was neither too hot nor too cold. It was just right for her, so she finished it all!

Then Goldilocks saw the three chairs. "I think I'll sit down and rest," she said. First, she tried Papa Bear's great big chair, but it was too hard for her. Next, she tried Mama Bear's middle-sized chair, but it was too soft for her. Then she tried Baby Bear's wee little chair. It was neither too hard nor too soft. It was just right. But the bottom of the chair fell out, and down she fell, *plunk*—on her own bottom!

So Goldilocks climbed the stairs. She went into the bears' bedroom, where she saw the three beds. First, she lay down in Papa Bear's great big bed. But it was too high for her. Then she lay down in Mama Bear's middle-sized bed. But it was also too high for her. Then she lay down in Baby Bear's wee little bed. It was just right for her. So she curled up and went to sleep.

When the three bears knew their porridge would be cool enough to eat, they came home for breakfast. Papa Bear looked into his great big bowl. Then he growled, in his great big voice,

"Someone has been eating my porridge!"

Mama Bear looked into her middle-sized bowl. And she said, in her middle-sized voice,

"Someone has been eating *my* porridge!"

Then Baby Bear looked into his wee little bowl. He cried out, in his wee little voice,

"Someone has been eating *my* porridge, and has eaten it all up!"

Papa Bear saw that the cushion on his great big chair
was out of place. He growled, in his great big voice,
"Someone has been sitting in my chair!"

Then Mama Bear looked at her middle-sized chair,
and she said, in her middle-sized voice,

"Someone has been sitting in *my* chair!"

Then Baby Bear looked at his wee little chair. He cried out, in his wee little voice,

"Someone has been sitting in *my* chair, and has broken it!"

The three bears went up and looked in the bedroom.
Papa Bear saw that the pillow was not in place on his
great big bed. He growled, in his great big voice,

"Someone has been lying in my bed!"

Then Mama Bear saw that the pillow was out of place on her middle-sized bed. She said, in her middle-sized voice,

"Someone has been lying in *my* bed!"

Then Baby Bear looked at his wee little bed. His pillow was right in its place. But on his pillow rested the head of a little girl—it was Goldilocks! So Baby Bear cried out, in his wee little voice,

"Someone has been lying in *my* bed, and she is still here!"

Now in her sleep, Goldilocks had heard the great big voice of Papa Bear, but she thought it was the rumble of thunder and the roar of rain. She had also heard the middle-sized voice of Mama Bear and thought it was only a voice in a dream. But when she heard Baby Bear's wee little voice, it was so shrill and sharp that she awakened at once.

Goldilocks sat up and
looked around the room.

As soon as she saw the three bears, she tumbled out
of bed and stumbled to the window. Then she jumped
out and ran into the woods.

The three bears went to the window and called, "Come back! Come back!" But that was the last they ever saw of Goldilocks.